DRUG DANGERS

ECSTASY
and Other Designer
DRUG DANGERS

Myra Weatherly

Enslow Publishers, Inc.

40 Industrial Road   PO Box 38
Box 398   Aldershot
Berkeley Heights, NJ 07922   Hants GU12 6BP
USA   UK

http://www.enslow.com

Library of Congress Cataloging-in-Publication Data

Weatherly, Myra.
    Ecstasy and other designer drug dangers / Myra Weatherly.
        p. cm. — (Drug dangers)
    Includes bibliographical references and index.
    Summary: Presents the dangers of ecstasy, crystal meth, crank, and
other designer drugs, discussing their effects and addictive nature and
the treatment of their abuse.
    ISBN 0-7660-1322-7
    1. Designer drugs Juvenile literature. 2. MDMA (Drug) Juvenile
literature. [1. Designer drugs. 2. Drugs. 3. Drug abuse.]
    I. Title. II. Series.
    RM316.W43   2000
    362.29'9-dc21   99-39200
                                                CIP

Printed in the United States of America

10 9 8 7 6 5 4 3 2 1

To Our Readers:
All Internet addresses in this book were active and appropriate when we
went to press. Any comments or suggestions can be sent by e-mail to
Comments@enslow.com or to the address on the back cover.

contents

1 Real-Life Stories 5

2 Social Issues 8

3 Young People and
Designer Drugs 24

4 Physical and Chemical
Effects of Abuse 27

5 Fighting Drug Abuse 48

Questions for Discussion 55

Chapter Notes 56

Where to Write 60

Glossary 62

Further Reading 63

Index 64

Titles in the **Drug Dangers** series:

Alcohol Drug Dangers
ISBN 0-7660-1159-3

Amphetamine Drug Dangers
ISBN 0-7660-1321-9

Crack and Cocaine Drug Dangers
ISBN 0-7660-1155-0

Diet Pill Drug Dangers
ISBN 0-7660-1158-5

Ecstasy and Other Designer Drug Dangers
ISBN 0-7660-1322-7

Herbal Drug Dangers
ISBN 0-7660-1319-7

Heroin Drug Dangers
ISBN 0-7660-1156-9

Inhalant Drug Dangers
ISBN 0-7660-1153-4

LSD, PCP, and Hallucinogen Drug Dangers
ISBN 0-7660-1318-9

Marijuana Drug Dangers
ISBN 0-7660-1214-X

Speed and Methamphetamine Drug Dangers
ISBN 0-7660-1157-7

Steroid Drug Dangers
ISBN 0-7660-1154-2

Tobacco and Nicotine Drug Dangers
ISBN 0-7660-1317-0

Tranquilizer, Barbiturate, and Downer
Drug Dangers
ISBN 0-7660-1320-0

one

Real-Life Stories

Nancy snorted crystal meth for the first time at a party. Other people were doing it. Why not give it a try? At the time, she was a sophomore in high school. In the beginning, she liked it because it made her talk a lot. Being able to go for days without sleep also seemed cool. But when she *did* sleep, she felt miserable afterward.

Nancy lost so much weight that her cheeks sunk in and her ribs stuck out—side effects of crystal meth. People bombarded her with questions. Why are you so skinny? What's the matter with you? They did not know she was using crystal meth. Neither did her mom. She had no idea that Nancy's skipping school was drug related.

What started out as a weekend thing for Nancy turned out to be an everyday thing. For about four months, she used crystal meth all the time. She began hallucinating—seeing and talking to people who were not there.

When she did not have crystal meth, Nancy lashed out at her friends and hated herself for doing so. When she began throwing up blood and the crystal meth, she decided to get help. Warned that she would die if she did not stop using crystal, Nancy suffered through the horrible process of kicking the habit.

These days Nancy says, "I don't do drugs now. I think my experience with crystal made me realize that bad things do happen when you do drugs. All of a sudden, it smacks you in the face."[1]

Seventeen-year-old Travis's grades were failing. He had trouble eating and sleeping. His baffled parents asked him about drug abuse. He confessed to trying crank. The next day his parents suffered a bigger blow when they found out Travis had been high on crank when he confessed.

Two days later, Travis broke a girl's jaw. His parents still did not link his wild behavior with steady drug use, but they did seek help at a school clinic. Travis convinced the counselor that he had stopped using crank.

The truth was that he was hooked. His addiction took a turn for the worse, resulting in his being thrown out of school for cutting classes. In the months that followed, Travis turned into an angry, quick-to-fight teen. At their wits' end, his parents gave him a choice: either follow their rules or move out.

A few weeks later, Travis was dead.

He had spent ten days in the hospital with flulike symptoms that turned out to be a rare form of meningitis. Meningitis is a disease that affects the membranes covering the brain and the spinal cord. Drug abuse had made his body so weak that he could no longer fight off this dangerous illness.

Already grieving over the loss of Travis, his parents became more upset when they learned that their older son had introduced crank to his brother. They placed the blame on their lack of parenting skills. "Travis said 'crank,' but we didn't investigate it enough. . . . If we had, Travis would be alive today," said his father.[2]

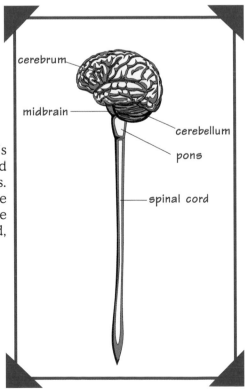

cerebrum

midbrain

cerebellum

pons

spinal cord

Drug abuse made Travis's body so weak that he could no longer fight off meningitis. This disease affects the membranes covering the brain and the spinal cord, and can be deadly.

two

Social
Issues

Nancy and Travis both used designer drugs. Street names for these illegally made drugs make them sound appealing to the likely drug user. These mysterious names tend to change quite often and vary by region. Names such as ecstasy, china white, and crystal promise a glamorous life. Yet designer drugs have destroyed thousands of lives.

Who Uses These Drugs?

Use of designer drugs is widespread among teenagers, college students, and young adults. Some young people consider designer drugs safe. Not true. These drugs with the cool street names are dangerous, addictive—even deadly.

Encouraging news comes from the 1998 Monitoring the Future Study of nearly fifty thousand American high school students. Investigators

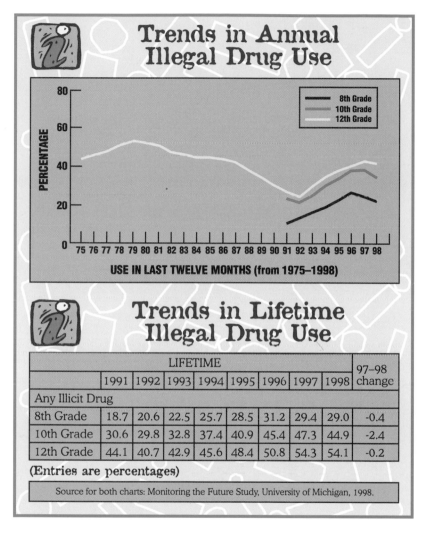

Trends in Annual Illegal Drug Use

8th Grade
10th Grade
12th Grade

USE IN LAST TWELVE MONTHS (from 1975–1998)

Trends in Lifetime Illegal Drug Use

	LIFETIME								97–98 change
	1991	1992	1993	1994	1995	1996	1997	1998	
Any Illicit Drug									
8th Grade	18.7	20.6	22.5	25.7	28.5	31.2	29.4	29.0	-0.4
10th Grade	30.6	29.8	32.8	37.4	40.9	45.4	47.3	44.9	-2.4
12th Grade	44.1	40.7	42.9	45.6	48.4	50.8	54.3	54.1	-0.2

(Entries are percentages)

Source for both charts: Monitoring the Future Study, University of Michigan, 1998.

note that although the improvement is modest, the use of illegal drugs—including designer drugs—by this population is finally heading downward after six years of steady increases.

Why Do People Use These Drugs?

Most people do not use drugs. They would not risk hurting their bodies, family, friends, or performance at

Users of designer drugs may mistakenly believe that these drugs are safe alternatives to cocaine (shown above) and heroin (shown below). Unfortunately, this assumption can sometimes have deadly consequences.

school or work. However, some people turn to drug abuse as a way of life. A person's need to be independent can have positive aspects, but it can also lead to drug experimentation. Some people may try drugs out of curiosity. Sometimes people act on any idea that pops into their head. Not thinking of the consequences of drug use may lead to disaster. Users of designer drugs find them less expensive and easier to get than the drugs they mimic. They believe that designer drugs are safe alternatives to drugs like cocaine or heroin, but they could not be more wrong.

To Be Accepted

It is normal to want to be popular. But some people get into the drug habit thinking it will help them to be liked by others. Users of the designer drug ecstasy report feeling close to others. Many teens start using drugs because they are pressured by a friend or acquaintance. They fear that their peers will not like them if they refuse. In some schools and communities, it is the "in" thing to do. Some young people mistakenly think that all the cool people are doing drugs.

To Overcome Boredom

Young people may use drugs because they feel their lives are boring. They yearn for excitement. They may turn to crystal methamphetamine for excitement. Users hear and see things that are not there. Moving things seem to have a tail like a comet—even a moving hand or a moving car has a tail. After the rush is over, however, users not only still face the problem of boredom but a host of other problems as well.

Users of crystal methamphetamine may see and hear things that are not there. The reality around them can become distorted and confusing.

To Escape From Problems

Some people use drugs thinking the drugs will help them to deal with problems. They want to make unpleasant feelings go away. For a brief period, people who use china white, for instance, feel wonderful. Their problems seem to go away. Drugs merely hide problems, however. Eventually drug users end up with more problems than they had before they started doing drugs. Drug-addicted teens may steal to support their habit. Drugs are not the solution to problems.

To Satisfy an Addiction

Some people use designer drugs because what started as a curiosity has turned into a habit they cannot kick. They are "hooked"—addicted to the drug. Every designer drug has the potential to kill the user. Why would anyone take a chance on dying?

Whatever the reason may be, people use illegal drugs worldwide—beginning in the preteen and teenage years in many instances.

Ecstasy

Ecstasy is the most commonly used street name for the drug known as MDMA (3,4-methylenedioxymethamphetamine). Other nicknames for this compound are X, E, Adam, essence, Eve, XTC, and rhapsody.

This laboratory-made drug, which comes in white powder, tablets, or capsules, is popular with young people who like to dance at raves—all-night party

How to Recognize Signs of Abuse

Signs of abuse include
- agitation—A state of nervousness and confusion;
- decreased appetite;
- euphoria—a sense of extreme well-being;
- excessive talking;
- hallucinations—hearing and seeing things that are not really there;
- mood swings—wide variations in mood-from extremely happy to extremely sad and back again;
- paranoia; and
- sleeplessness.

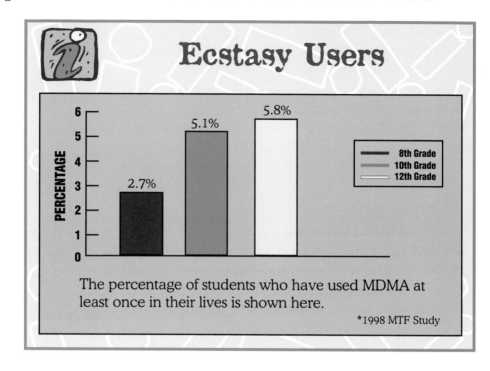

Ecstasy Users

8th Grade — 2.7%
10th Grade — 5.1%
12th Grade — 5.8%

The percentage of students who have used MDMA at least once in their lives is shown here.

*1998 MTF Study

sessions held in abandoned warehouses or other out-of-the-way places. About 35 percent of teenagers say that ecstasy is "easy to get."[1] They take it at parties and on weekends with friends. Ecstasy may be found in clubs and at rock concerts.

How can you tell if someone is getting high on ecstasy? It is not always easy. However, there are telltale signs that point to the possibility. Change of personality and a new set of friends should be warning signs. Other signs of ecstasy use include

- ◆ agitation
- ◆ blurred vision
- ◆ chills or sweating
- ◆ involuntary teeth grinding
- ◆ loss in interest in school, friends, and hobbies

- panic attacks
- pleasure-seeking behavior
- short attention span
- sleep problems
- upset stomach
- weight loss

Methamphetamine

What would you think if you saw people scratching their skin nonstop to get rid of imagined insects? Weird, no doubt. Users of meth have delusions of insects on their skin. They may pull out their hair and act out violently.

Methamphetamine may look like white powder or glasslike shards, and it enables people to work for days on end without sleep. Truck drivers trying to stay awake on long trips and students cramming for exams may use methamphetamine.

On the street, users are known as tweakers. They are easy to spot. Sunken eyes, caved-in chest, puppetlike motions, and agitated behavior are common symptoms.

Users in clinical and hospital settings are called methamphetamine addicts. "They look like every ounce of life has been drained from them, and they are still walking," said Connie Johnson, a Minneapolis drug-treatment counselor.[2]

Said Dr. Larry McEvoy, an emergency room doctor in Billings, Montana:

> I've seen fourteen-year-old girls with infected arms who have been stuck a bunch of times by people who aren't very good at hitting veins. And I'm frequently surprised by the number of people who don't use it every day but don't feel bad about dabbling in it. They

Users of methamphetamine may imagine that they have bugs crawling on their skin, despite the fact that the bugs do not exist.

seem to be unaware of the precipice they're hanging over.[3]

Other warning signs of methamphetamine abuse often include

- ◆ bad breath
- ◆ blurred vision
- ◆ coughing
- ◆ enlarged pupils in the eyes
- ◆ irritability
- ◆ loss of appetite
- ◆ sinus infections
- ◆ violence for no reason
- ◆ weight loss

Methamphetamine abuse often leads to car crashes and crimes. Fires can result from explosions in makeshift laboratories. Fumes that come as a result of making methamphetamine may lead to death for those who sniff them.

Joseph, a three-year-old Arizona boy, fell asleep on the couch in his home. He died after being overcome by fumes seeping into the living room. The fumes came from a secret laboratory, operating in the next room.[4]

In addition, illegal meth labs are not operated with much regard for environmental safety. "Meth makers toss their byproducts into the garbage, down the drain or into trenches, creating the potential for contaminating water and poisoning people and pets."[5]

Methamphetamine abuse can lead to explosions in illegal laboratories like the one shown here.

MPTP

In the summer of 1982, six young heroin addicts ended up in emergency rooms in the San Francisco area. They displayed the same bizarre and mysterious symptoms—their bodies were so stiff that they seemed to be frozen. These "frozen" patients were fully conscious but unable to speak or move.

Neurosurgeon J. William Langston diagnosed the six young men and women as having advanced Parkinson's disease. But how could that be? Parkinson's disease is a disease that weakens the muscles in the body, and is normally confined to the elderly. Acting as a medical detective, Dr. Langston determined that the patients had all used the same tainted batch of synthetic heroin—MPTP. Eventually, he "thawed out" three of the six—George, Anita, and Connie.

Their astonishing recovery attracted worldwide press coverage and led to an explosion of research, giving hope to millions who suffer from Parkinson's and other

 Signs of Use of MPTP

- ◆ drooling

- ◆ drowsiness

- ◆ mental confusion

- ◆ progressive freezing of bodily functions—only breathing, hearing, seeing, and thinking continue

- ◆ uncontrollable shaking of the arms and legs

degenerative brain disorders. Dr. Langston recounts his efforts to find a solution in *The Case of the Frozen Addicts*.[6]

MPPP (a form of MPTP) was designed to replace heroin. Its chemical structure is closely related to that of the drug Demerol™, prescribed by doctors to relieve pain. The process of making MPPP requires cooking many chemicals together for a long time at a constant temperature. Excessive heat results in the drug becoming a deadly poison—MPTP. When injected into the body, MPTP travels straight to the brain, destroying nerve cells. Some victims die with the needle still in their arm.

Special K

Two teenagers in Nashua, New Hampshire, broke into thirteen veterinary hospitals, hunting for a drug. As unbelievable as it sounds, the drug was an animal tranquilizer, ketamine, a white powder also known on the street as special k, k, or breakfast cereal.[7] Ketamine can be snorted into the nostrils, smoked, or dissolved in water for drinking.

In 1995, the U.S. Drug Enforcement Administration added special k to its list of new and dangerous drugs. The office reported finding the drug "all over" the nation and issued a warning that use is increasing at teen rave parties.

Special k causes hallucinations, a drunken state, numbness of hands and feet, and loss of muscle control. London researcher Karl Jansen compared the brain's chemical reaction to the drug to a "near death experience."[8] Ketamine may cause users to vomit or pass out. Users may also be unable to speak or feel pain. Large doses can be fatal.

John Lily, a scientist who studied the body's nervous

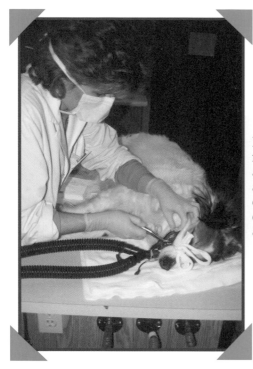

Ketamine is a drug that is meant to be used as an animal tranquilizer. It can, also, be smoked, snorted, or dissolved into water for drinking by users in search of a high.

system and pioneered communications with dolphins, took ketamine in the 1970s. He began using it, hoping it would cure his migraine headaches. At one point, he believed that he was a visitor to earth from the year 3001. He even imagined talking with the aliens. Lily abused this drug for decades.[9]

CAT

One of the more recent designer drugs to hit the United States is methcathinone, also known as CAT, Cadillac express, Jeff, goob, mulka, or wild cat. CAT is a laboratory-made white powder—a version of meth-amphetamine and cathinone. The drug cathinone is a stimulant found in khat, a plant grown in Africa and southern Arabia.

In 1989, a University of Michigan student discovered documentation and samples of methcathinone, dating to the 1950s. Because of the dangerous and addictive nature of the drug, the study was abandoned. Using the recipe found in the records, the amateur chemist mixed a substitute for khat. In 1991, he began selling the CAT that he made in his home lab.[10] Chemicals used in CAT are the same chemicals that are used in asthma and cold medications, paint solvent, household cleaners, auto battery acid, Drano™, and paint thinner.

As hard as it seems to believe, this "witches brew" of deadly ingredients quickly spread through the Midwest and into other parts of the country as more people learned to make it.

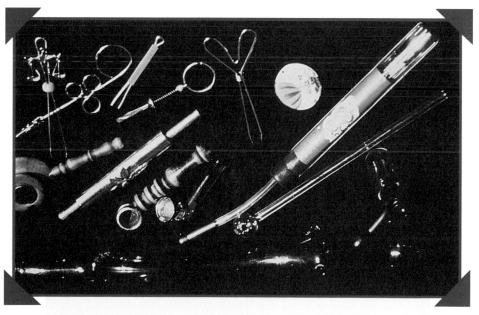

CAT is a designer form of cathinone, a stimulant found in the khat plant that grows in Africa and southern Arabia. It can be taken by using drug paraphernalia like the items shown here.

Some Facts on CAT

How Is It Used?	Effects of Use
◆ by mouth ◆ injected ◆ mixed in a liquid ◆ smoked in a pipe ◆ snorted	◆ anxiety ◆ burst of energy ◆ convulsions ◆ feelings of euphoria ◆ hallucinations ◆ increase in heart rate ◆ insomnia ◆ paranoia ◆ weight loss

Society and Drug Abuse

Young people are being exposed to drug use at increasingly young ages. Tools and resources must be made available to young people to aid them in making the right choices to remain drug-free.

Mixed Messages

Society and the mass media convey mixed messages about drug use. Young people find it hard to know what to believe or whom to believe. What can be done? Young people not only must know the facts, but also must learn how to put this knowledge to use.

A study by the national Drug Abuse Warning Network (DAWN) reported that deaths and emergency room visits related to the use of methamphetamines tripled from 1993 to 1997.

Yet teens are bombarded in music videos and other media by songs glamorizing drugs such as crystal meth.

Despite the fact that society keeps sending mixed messages, designer drugs are erratic, risky, and can be deadly.

Costs to Society

The Office of National Drug Policy reported that between 1988 and 1995 illegal drugs and the problems associated with them cost Americans $57.3 billion.[11] Drug-related crime accounted for more than half the estimated costs. These costs also included lost time from jobs as a result of drug-related illness as well as health care expenses.

Illegal drug use places students at risk of dropping out of school or college. Loss of human potential, premature deaths, and drug-related deaths all negatively affect society.

Contributing Factors to Increased Drug-Related Costs

◆ the epidemic of heavy cocaine use;

◆ the HIV/AIDS epidemic;

◆ an eightfold increase of prison costs for drug offenses; and

◆ a threefold increase in crimes related to drugs.[12]

In 1998, Barry McCaffrey, director of the White House Office of National Drug Control Policy, stated that drug-related illness, death, and crime cost the nation $66.9 billion each year and some fourteen thousand lives.[13]

three

Young People and Designer Drugs

Brian Harvey was the lead singer of East 17, a successful British band in the 1990s. He lost his job after he promoted ecstasy and admitted that he had used the drug. Radio stations stopped playing his records. His dismissal from the band was supported by the prime minister.[1]

Real-Life Stories

Erin was introduced to crank in her sophomore year by her two best friends. She had already tried other drugs, and she was curious to try some of the white powder.

That first try led to snorting crank every weekend. Erin liked the carefree feelings and alertness produced by the drug. She recalled being happy that she no longer had a weight problem.

What If . . .

What If:

- What if an older brother was using drugs?
- What if a friend's parents were using drugs?
- What if objectionable music (praising drugs) was being played on a favorite radio station? What could be done?
- What if a party turned out not to be a drug-free social event?
- What if a friend was doing drugs?
- What if a friend began dealing drugs?

These questions will help to find out if drugs are affecting a friend or relative.

- Has there been a sudden drop in grades—without reasonable explanation?
- Has this person's circle of friends changed?
- Have there been any instances of theft?
- Does this person suffer from intense sadness?
- Does this person see things that are not there?
- Does this person become violent for little or no reason?
- Does this person feel happy one moment and sad the next?
- Does this person ever miss school due to drugs?
- Has anyone in this person's family ever had a problem with drugs?

Weekend use soon became a daily habit for Erin. To support her expensive habit, she became a dealer. She sold her stash to regular customers in the girls' bathroom at Las Lomas High, just outside San Francisco.

"I was tempted to make a business of it, but after awhile I was using more than I was selling," she said. "I'd lost control."

Paranoia, delusions, and out-of-body experiences replaced her feelings of alertness and well-being. She picked at imaginary dots on her skin. Her diet consisted of two crackers a day and a candy bar. Instead of graduating from high school, Erin found herself in a rehabilitation center on the rough road back from being a crank addict.[2]

Christie, a sixteen-year-old from Miami, started experimenting with drugs at the age of seven. She told her story on a national television program, "Designer Drugs Designed for Dopes." By the age of eleven, she was doing the animal tranquilizer known as ketamine, or special k. She did not have to buy special k—her older friends gave her the hallucinogenic drug.

Christie would like help to combat her problem. But it will be difficult without a strong support system. At the time the show aired in 1996, she had a cocaine-addicted mother and no place to live.[3]

four

Physical and Chemical Effects of Abuse

Take a secret lab and an existing drug such as morphine or amphetamine. Add a couple of chemicals. Give that new substance a mysterious name. What do you have? A new designer drug.

These imitation drugs mixed by "bathtub chemists" can be much more potent than the real thing. Not only are these drugs dangerous in themselves, but a goof in the lab—such as overheating a substance—can mean death. Although designer drugs did not hit the streets with a bang until the 1980s, they have been around since the early part of the twentieth century.

The term *designer drug* was first used by Gary Henderson, a professor of pharmacology at the University of California, in the early 1980s to describe synthetic or laboratory-made drugs.[1] These drugs do not come from plants, as does heroin, for example, which is made from poppies. Designer drugs are made by people in illegal laboratories. These drugs consist of copycat chemicals designed to mimic illegal drugs. They are usually more powerful than the original drug.[2]

How Designer Drugs Got Their Start

In the late 1970s, underground chemists began manufacturing synthetic substances in secret labs—as a way of going around existing drug laws. These new drugs remained legal until the 1980s. Federal drug laws were changed in 1986 to include any analogs—substances that are chemically similar to one another—of a controlled substance under Schedule I of the Controlled Substances Act.

Anyone in possession of a Schedule I drug faces severe federal penalties—up to one year in prison and/or a fine up to five thousand dollars for the first offense. The second offense carries a ten thousand dollars fine and up to two years in prison.

The punishment for making and selling Schedule I drugs is imprisonment for up to twenty years and/or a fine of up to one million dollars.

Even stiffer penalties are imposed for the following:

- ◆ repeated offenses;
- ◆ larger amounts of the substance;
- ◆ sale to a person under the age of eighteen or to a pregnant woman;
- ◆ serious injury or death resulting from distribution;
- ◆ sales within one thousand feet of a school ground, playground, youth center, swimming pool, or video arcade.[3]

Ecstasy

Ecstasy is a laboratory-made drug designed to produce the same effects as mescaline—a psychedelic drug made from the peyote cactus plant. Ecstasy combines the effects of stimulants and hallucinogens. Many people have reported a distortion of time perception.[4] Ecstasy produces a shorter high than other versions of psychedelic drugs, such as LSD. Ecstasy is the most commonly used name for the drug MDMA (3,4 methylenedioxymethamphetamine). Structurally, MDMA is similar to its parent compound, MDA. Both were synthesized at about the same time in the early 1900s.

MDMA was developed in 1914 by E. Merck and Company, a German pharmaceutical firm, prior to World War I. It remained a largely forgotten formula until the late 1970s, when it was prescribed for psychotherapy patients who were severely withdrawn.

Ecstasy emerged in the early 1980s as the "in" party drug. Since then, it has grown into an international youth phenomenon. From Great Britain, where raves—all-night dance parties with loud music and widespread ecstasy use—originated, this recreational drug quickly became the drug of choice for ravers in the Netherlands and North America.[5]

Ecstasy use is not limited to raves. Some people take the drug in smaller settings—with friends at someone's house. This does not, however, make the drug safer. The risk of serious consequences is the same—be it at a nightclub or at home.

MDMA use has been responsible for a variety of psychological problems. People who have taken repeated high doses of MDMA, have reported panic attacks. The attacks usually end for most users when they stop using MDMA. However, for a few, the panic attacks can go on for months. Other chronic, high-dose users have had hallucinations. They may also exhibit symptoms of paranoia, a mental disorder. People who are paranoid are extremely suspicious, have delusions, or feel persecuted. These symptoms go away when the drug is stopped.[6]

In 1985, the Drug Enforcement Administration (DEA) banned MDMA and placed it in Schedule I, the most restrictive category of illegal drugs. This classification was based on laboratory findings that MDA—a chemical cousin to MDMA—caused brain damage in studies involving animals. Drugs in this category have a high potential for abuse, no accepted medical use, and no accepted safety even when used by a professional.

Ecstasy is a laboratory-made drug that produces the same effects as mescaline—a psychedelic drug that comes from the peyote cactus plant.

Making, selling, or possessing ecstasy in the United States is illegal.

MDMA is also a restricted drug in Canada. It is listed on Schedule H—drugs deemed to have no medical value—of Canada's Food and Drugs Act.[7] These restrictions in the United States and Canada, however, have failed to stem the rising tide of the popularity of ecstasy.

Methamphetamine

Methamphetamine, also known as meth, speed, crystal, glass, ice, or chalk, has a high potential for abuse and dependence.

Methamphetamine was developed in 1919 from its parent drug amphetamine. It was used in nasal sprays and inhalers for people with breathing problems. Methamphetamine is classified as a Schedule II drug.[8] It has a high potential for abuse and is available only through a prescription with no refills. It has limited medical use today.

Accepted Medical Use

- ◆ treats narcolepsy—A disorder that causes the affected person to fall asleep unexpectedly.
- ◆ treats attention deficit hyperactivity disorder (ADHD)—Difficulty focusing on tasks and paying attention.
- ◆ treats obesity—Excessive weight gain.

During World War II, methamphetamine was used by the soldiers of many countries to prevent tiredness. At the end of World War II, methamphetamine abuse reached epidemic proportions in Japan when military supplies of the drug were released to the public.

In the 1950s and 1960s, methamphetamine was widely available through prescriptions and rapidly growing illegal sources. Abuse by such groups as students, sports figures, and long-distance truckers led to tighter restrictions in the 1970s. Use decreased for a while.

Laws have not stopped the illegal production of methamphetamine. By the 1980s, speed was back in the news. What started out as a drug problem in sections of the West and Southwest quickly spread across the country, particularly to urban and rural sections of the South and Midwest. Availability and use of methamphetamines soared in the 1990s. Users seem to see the drug as fashionable and safe. They tend to ignore the fact that speed can kill.

China White

It began like any other Friday night in a certain neighborhood of New York, with drug dealers on street corners. Dealers were selling a new drug called tango and cash. And cash was the name of the game, as the drug dealers quickly sold their goods and then fled the streets.

A few hours later, the first overdoses started turning up in emergency rooms in New York City, New Jersey, and Connecticut. What began as an ordinary Friday night turned into a nightmare. By the end of the weekend, 12 people were dead and 136 were hospitalized in three states—all victims of tango and cash. One junkie died with the syringe delivering the dose still hanging from his arm. These victims had overdosed on synthetic heroin.

This designer drug was sold from a single block in the South Bronx.[9]

Tango and cash, china white, mexican brown, and new heroin are fentanyl analogs. Fentanyl was developed in Europe in 1968. Because it is a powerful and short-acting pain reliever, fentanyl is used in hospitals for a number of surgical procedures. "Drugs from the fentanyl series are excellent heroin substitutes because they work just like heroin to block pain and cause euphoria."[10] But there is one major difference—china white and other fentanyl look-alikes are eight to one thousand times more potent than heroin.

China white is designed in illegal laboratories. It looks and acts exactly like heroin. It first appeared on the streets of southern California in 1979. Overdoses, deaths, poisonings, and addictions soon followed. An article reporting an outbreak of overdoses of fentanyl analogs in Pennsylvania was published in a 1991 issue of the *Journal of the American Medical Association.*[11]

While house-sitting for some friends, a nineteen-year-old California girl found a stash of drugs. She snorted some of the white powder. She did not know that the powder was a batch of a fentanyl analog. When the owners of the home returned, they discovered her body. A DEA agent concluded that the young girl probably thought it was cocaine. But what she "snorted was a load of dynamite."[12]

China white (alpha-methylfentanyl) was placed on Schedule I of the Controlled Substances Act in 1982. Unfortunately, as soon as one heroin substitute is outlawed, another one appears on the street with the potential to be deadly. The number of spin-offs of synthetic drugs is almost unlimited.[13]

Groups of Designer Drugs

Designer drugs fall into three major groups: stimulants, hallucinogens, and opiates.

Stimulants include the group of drugs that increase alertness and a sense of well-being. They also reduce tiredness and appetite. Hallucinogens change the way we see things, think, and feel. Opiates are painkillers that cause extreme happiness followed by sleepiness. There are some overlapping characteristics in these groups.

Designer Stimulants

Designer stimulants enter the brain quickly. They produce effects similar to the body's own naturally occurring stimulants. Illegal stimulants cause bodily reactions to speed up, increasing heartbeat, blood pressure, and energy. Stimulant drugs fill the brain with false feelings of extreme happiness and power.

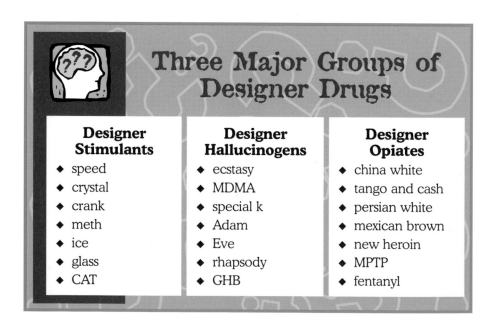

Three Major Groups of Designer Drugs

Designer Stimulants	Designer Hallucinogens	Designer Opiates
◆ speed	◆ ecstasy	◆ china white
◆ crystal	◆ MDMA	◆ tango and cash
◆ crank	◆ special k	◆ persian white
◆ meth	◆ Adam	◆ mexican brown
◆ ice	◆ Eve	◆ new heroin
◆ glass	◆ rhapsody	◆ MPTP
◆ CAT	◆ GHB	◆ fentanyl

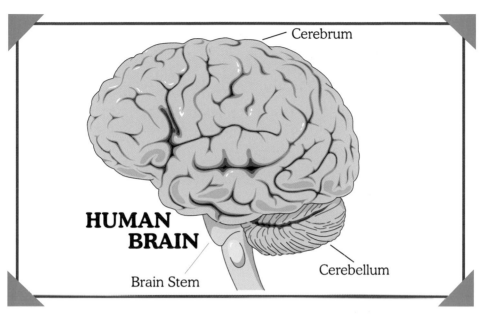

Cerebrum

HUMAN
BRAIN

Brain Stem

Cerebellum

This drawing of a brain shows its major regions.

The brain is made up of three main parts: the cerebrum, the cerebellum, and the brain stem. Each region of the brain is responsible for a particular function. The brain controls and directs all the muscles and organs in the body.

The largest part of the brain, the cerebrum, is the thinking part of the brain. The cerebrum allows humans to see, hear, taste, smell, touch, solve problems, and remember things.

Underneath the cerebrum is the cerebellum. This part of the brain allows the body's muscles to work together smoothly and helps to maintain balance. The cerebellum allows people to do many things without having to think about them.

The brain stem connects the brain to the spinal cord. The brain and spinal cord make up the central nervous system. The brain stem is like a busy intersection with nerves—fine threads that carry information to different parts of the body—speeding back and forth between the brain and the spinal cord. Every second, the brain stem sifts through millions of signals to determine which signals will be sent on to the higher centers of the brain. Also, many basic life functions such as heart rate, breathing, eating, and sleeping are controlled by the brain stem.

How Does Methamphetamine Work in the Body?

Methamphetamine stimulates the central nervous system. The wave of artificial happiness may last from four to thirty hours. Gradually the euphoria wears off, and the user is left feeling very sad and jittery.

Chronic users go through a number of stages when they are on a binge—using heavily and consistently. The most dangerous stage is called tweaking. Tweakers are users who have not slept for days and are paranoid and hostile. Their craving for another hit of methamphetamine often leads to unpredictable and violent behavior.

An Arizona man high on methamphetamines hacked his son's head off and tossed it out the window of his van. The father had stopped along the side of a busy highway and stabbed fourteen-year-old Eric in the neck and throat about sixty times before throwing the head out the window about a mile down the highway.

Eric's younger brother, Larry, was in the van at the time of the murder. He ran away and told authorities that his father had been on methamphetamines and became furious when he ran out of the drugs.[14]

Effects of Designer Stimulants on the Mind

◆ aggressive and violent behavior

◆ extreme sadness

◆ false sense of confidence and power

◆ moodiness and irritability

◆ panic

◆ paranoia—feeling that everyone is out to get the user

◆ talking excessively

What Are the Effects of Designer Stimulants on the Body?

In addition to changing the way the brain works, stimulant drugs speed up the body's functions. Users run the risks of vitamin and mineral deficiencies, lowered resistance to disease, and organ damage.

Snorting methamphetamine irritates the pathways in the nose. This irritation causes the user to have a constant runny nose. Nausea is usually associated with swallowing methamphetamine. Some people, not wanting to irritate their nose or experience nausea, resort to injecting methamphetamine. Repeated use of a needle, however, can lead to collapsed veins and the risk of becoming infected with the AIDS virus. Users who smoke ice—crystallized methamphetamine—put their health at risk by exposing their lung tissue to fumes from meth crystals.

An overdose is possible no matter which form of methamphetamine is used. No matter what it is called or how it gets into the body, methamphetamine can be deadly.

Physical Consequences of Methamphetamine Abuse

- breathing problems
- dry, itchy skin
- inability to sleep
- increased heart rate and blood pressure
- kidney and lung disorders
- liver damage
- loss of appetite
- numbness
- weight loss

Designer Stimulants and Pregnancy

Methamphetamine abuse during pregnancy may result in premature delivery of the fetus or even death. Babies born to methamphetamine-addicted mothers tend to be incapable of bonding. They have been known to cry for twenty-four hours without stopping, and to have tremors. They may have glassy eyes, low muscle tone, and poor feeding habits. Research indicates that methamphetamine may be linked to birth defects.[15]

Children at Risk

Children born to parents who use speed are at an increased risk of child abuse and neglect.

It was the day after Christmas. Boom! Boom! Boom!

An explosion rocked a small town in southern California. A large mobile home burst into flames. Kathy James, her seven-year-old son, Jimmy, and two men escaped the inferno. But trapped inside and screaming in terror were Kathy James's three younger children.

Horrified neighbors found it strange that the mother did not want anyone to call for help. By the time firefighters arrived, she and the other survivors had disappeared. Rescuers found the charred bodies of three-year-old Deon, two-year-old Jackson, and one-year-old Megan. After sifting through the debris, investigators determined that Kathy James had been "cooking up" methamphetamine in her kitchen when the explosion occurred.

"Maybe the legacy of the three James children can wake the country up to the dangers of meth-amphetamine. I sure hope so," said a special narcotics agent at the time of the tragedy.[16]

Withdrawal Symptoms

There are a number of symptoms that occur when a consistent user stops using methamphetamines. These symptoms include an intense craving for the drug, extreme sadness, mental confusion, violent behavior, inability to sleep, and tiredness.

An addict may experience these withdrawal symptoms for a while, but the benefits of a longer, healthier, and more fulfilling life far outweigh an addiction to methamphetamines.

"You may not have heard of a drug called crank, crystal, speed, or ice. But if someone ever offers it to you, run as fast as you can. I tried it twice and ended up being addicted for nine months. And if you think you might not ever be offered it, think again. If it happened to me, a middle-class midwestern mother, it can happen to anyone," said Maryann.[17]

Maryann married as soon as she graduated from high school to get away from her abusive father. Ten years and two kids later, she was divorced. A second marriage proved to be an even bigger mistake. Despite her unhappy private life, she enjoyed a very successful career until she started seeing Roger, a childhood friend.

She soon learned that Roger was addicted to drugs. She had never smoked a cigarette, much less used drugs. From a few hits, Maryann's drug use increased until she was inhaling crank several times a day.

She even stole a coworker's credit card to pay her debts. After being confronted, she went home and confessed to her teenage children—who had no idea she was abusing drugs. Then she checked into a treatment center. Thanks to good therapy and the emotional support of her children, Maryann kicked her habit. "Throughout all this, there wasn't a day when I didn't crave the drug," she said.[18]

Drug addiction is a serious problem. Getting the next hit becomes the entire focus of an addict's life.

Designer Hallucinogens

Hallucinogens are a group of drugs that affect the brain. They distort the way the senses work and change impressions of time and space. People who use these drugs may not be able to tell the difference between reality and illusion.

Some hallucinogens can be found in plants. Certain types of mushrooms contain hallucinogenic chemicals. People have used hallucinogens for thousands of years.

Some hallucinogens can be found in plants. Certain types of mushrooms contain chemicals that cause hallucinations.

Ancient cultures, including Greece, Rome, Assyria, Persia, Mexico, and China, used hallucinogens in religious ceremonies, medicine, and witchcraft.

Researchers believe that hallucinogens were used by North American Indian tribes prior to the arrival of the first Europeans.[19] Not all hallucinogens come from natural substances, however. Some, such as ecstasy, special k, and CAT are made in laboratories.

Actions of Ecstasy in the Brain

Ecstasy (MDMA) can disrupt the brain's ability to communicate with the rest of the body. Ecstasy affects a chemical messenger in the brain that plays an important role in controlling sleep, emotions, and heart rate.

Dr. George Ricaurte at Johns Hopkins University

studied the effects of high doses of ecstasy on squirrel monkeys. Brain imaging techniques are now being used in clinical studies to determine the possibility of long-term brain damage in humans.[20]

Alan I. Leshner, director of the National Institute on Drug Abuse, issued a press release on December 21, 1998, about the findings of researchers at Johns Hopkins on memory problems caused by the drug ecstasy. "Not only does ecstasy cause problems while someone is using the drug, but it damages the brain in ways that can interfere with normal learning and memory that continue weeks after one stops taking it," said Leshner.

Physical Effects

The effects of ecstasy are unpredictable—depending on the dose, the strength, the user's mood, surroundings, and personality. Once in the body, the drug enters the bloodstream and is carried throughout the body. The first effects may be felt within thirty to ninety minutes and can last up to six hours. When an ecstasy high wears off, the user is extremely tired and very sad for days afterward.

Dangers Associated with Ecstasy

Some people feel anxious, confused, and paranoid while on the drug. Deep feelings of fear can lead to panic attacks. Such attacks can affect the ability to think clearly or make good judgments. Ecstasy tricks the mind into seeing things differently from the way they are. This distortion may affect coordination and lead to serious injury. Frequent use may cause liver and kidney damage and psychosis—a mental condition characterized by the loss of reality.

Physical Symptoms of Ecstasy Abuse

- ◆ blurred vision
- ◆ chills
- ◆ dilated pupils
- ◆ dryness of the mouth
- ◆ faintness
- ◆ increased heart rate, blood pressure, and body temperature
- ◆ jaw clenching
- ◆ muscle tension
- ◆ numbness of arms and legs
- ◆ sweating, nausea, vomiting, drooling

Negative reactions from hallucinogen use put young people at risk as they enter puberty—a time of rapid physical and emotional changes. Users may experience severe injuries, burns, falls, and car accidents. Before reaching adolescence, young people need to know the dangers of drug use and learn how to put this knowledge to use.

Mixing ecstasy with other drugs or substances results in even more unpredictable reactions. Users may take an ecstasy pill, not knowing that it has been "laced" with another legal or illegal drug. There is no way to tell how strong a pill is by sight. The only way to tell what is in an ecstasy pill is to have it tested. Ecstasy testing kits are being marketed in Britain—but not with the approval of the British government. Officials there see them as an "illegal moneymaking venture."[21]

Seizures, coma, and death may result from high doses. Deaths associated with ecstasy use are often due to heatstroke, as a result of the crowded, hot conditions at rave clubs.

Special K

Special k—ketamine hydrochloride—was developed as a surgical anesthetic. It is a powerful hallucinogen in addition to having anesthetic properties. Today, ketamine is used mostly by veterinarians as a tranquilizer in animal surgery.

Pharmaceutical ketamine is a liquid. Dealers cook the liquid until it is dry, then crush it into a powder. It is sold on the street as special k, k, or vitamin k. Powdered ketamine was used throughout the 1970s and 1980s. But it hit the rave scene big time in the 1990s.

The body of eighteen-year-old Donald Matthews was discovered outside a shopping mall in Fitchburg, Massachusetts. He was an apparent victim of a drug overdose of a mixture of special k and heroin. A girl who attended the same party where Matthews was last seen ended up in the hospital.[22]

Across the country, the drug has become a part of the scene at all-night dance parties for teens.

What Are the Effects of Special K?

Special k blocks chemical messengers (called transmitters) in the brain. When transmitters are out of balance, they may cause a person to see or hear things that are not there. They may also cause a person to become extremely happy, angry, afraid, or depressed. Users lose control of their thoughts and emotions.

Common side effects include amnesia, high blood pressure, slurred speech, aggressive behavior, impaired coordination, and potentially fatal breathing problems.

Ketamine's effects come on quickly—usually within fifteen seconds of injection or inhalation. Large doses produce out-of-body experiences—a feeling of being removed from one's own body, uncontrollable shaking, and flashbacks (recalling past experiences). Since ketamine is an anesthetic, it stops the user from feeling pain and may lead to serious personal injury. One gram of ketamine—a dose no larger than the size of a small piece of hard candy—can cause death.

GHB

GHB (Gamma hydroxybutyric acid) was first used by body builders to stimulate muscle growth. It is now used by young people on the club scene. GHB, which comes in both a liquid and a powder form, is made from a chemical used to clean circuit boards in computers. Because it is odorless and tasteless, GHB can be slipped into someone's drink without being noticed. There have been reports of GHB use in some rape cases. The Food and Drug Administration declared GHB illegal in 1990.

Negative Effects of GHB

- breathing problems that can be fatal
- comas
- liver failure
- seizures
- vomiting

Designer Opiates

Opiates are painkillers made from the seeds of Asian poppy plants. Opium, morphine, and codeine are all opiates. Abusers use these drugs for the extreme feelings of pleasure they produce. Opiates can also produce drowsiness and mental confusion. Use of opium for its pleasurable and painkilling effects dates to 4,000 B.C. Opium was an accepted part of ancient Greek medicine.

Opiates can cause physical and psychological addiction. Physical addiction occurs when the body cannot function properly without the drug. Constant use of opiates changes the way the addict's brain functions. Psychological addiction is a mental craving for the pleasure and escape from reality that the drug produces.

In the early 1800s, a German pharmacist developed

Opiates are painkillers made from the seeds of Asian poppy plants, like the ones shown here.

an opium preparation known as morphine—named after the Greek god of sleep. Morphine is an effective and highly addictive pain reliever. During the Civil War, morphine was used for the treatment of wounded soldiers. Heroin was developed in 1898 as a nonaddictive substitute for morphine. Heroin, however, turned out to be two and a half times more potent than morphine.

A Former Narcotics Addict's Story

Jack (not his real name), a graduate of a leading medical school, chose to specialize in anesthesiology specifically because it would enable him to get drugs easily. At first, he was hooked on cocaine. Then, he switched to morphine, a prescribed opiate that he got legally from the pharmacy.

"My world was hopeless, and I was helpless. . . . I had accepted the fact that I was doomed to die alone, in fear," said Jack of his addiction. "By that time, I was either on the street scoring, or in the hospital working as an emergency room physician."[23]

This shocking account is far from unusual. After going through a rehabilitation program, Jack kicked his habit and became a volunteer counselor to addicted doctors. He hopes to find a job in a hospital or clinic. Jack was one of the lucky ones.

The ingredients and strength of designer opiates are unpredictable. Overdosing on designer opiates causes the body to slow down and then come to a full stop—death.

five

Fighting
Drug Abuse

According to the 1998 Monitoring the Future Study, more than half (54.1 percent) of twelfth graders had used an illegal drug by the time they reached their senior year. That percentage had increased from 40.7 percent in 1992. Each year, the study surveys samples of American students in the eighth, tenth, and twelfth grades. Adolescent drug use is not limited to any one level of society. It cuts across gender and racial lines.

Abuse of any drug can have harmful effects. Abuse of designer drugs, however, poses a particular problem. Their effects are unpredictable, and they are not made with any particular care for safety. The consequences are often tragic.

The stories and the statistics are frightening. But it is encouraging to know that the war against drug abuse is being fought on many levels. Parents, teachers, students, law enforcement officials, the medical profession, community groups, the media, and federal, state, and local governments are all getting involved.

Innovative Programs

The treatment of drug abuse is difficult and costly. Prevention is much less expensive and easier to achieve. The following programs aim for prevention.

National Youth Anti-Drug Media Campaign

Since 1997, the Office of National Drug Control Policy (ONDCP) has been waging a large-scale media campaign to educate. The council hopes to show America's youth they can reject illegal drugs. This multifaceted prevention campaign is backed by some of America's major corporations and media companies. Nonprofit public and private organizations are also involved. The messages focus on preventing drug abuse before it starts and the benefits of staying drug-free. The National Youth Anti-Drug Media Campaign targets adolescents, ages nine to eighteen. This is the age range for the majority of beginning drug users.[1]

Mic Mac Theatre Group, Canada

Young people in Red Bank, New Brunswick, Canada, use drama to teach their peers about the dangers of drug abuse. The Mic Mac Theatre Group shared their unusual approach to drug prevention by presenting the drama "Total Eclipse of Addiction" at a recent meeting of the United Nations International Drug Control Program.[2]

Cultural Enhancement Through Storytelling

On the Tohono O'odham Indian Reservation near Tucson, Arizona, storytelling is used to create a strong sense of cultural identity. This strong sense of culture has been shown to help in resisting the temptation of drugs.[3]

Adolescent Substance Abuse Prevention

Medical students at the University of Chicago designed this school-based program. The students use science to educate fifth- to eighth-grade students about the dangers of drug abuse.[4]

Enhancing Emotional Competence

This prevention program for fourth graders in Oklahoma City teaches coping skills to those at risk. At-risk students include those who are victims of violence and/or emotional distress.[5]

Teen Challenge in Canada

For over twenty-five years, Teen Challenge has provided information and counseling against drug abuse in Canada. Teen Challenge Farm, a national farm treatment center near London, Ontario, Canada, helps young people get off drugs and stay free of addictions.[6]

Girl Power!

In November 1996, the Department of Health and Human Resources launched Girl Power!, a national campaign. This program is designed to teach girls between the ages of nine and fourteen about the dangers of substance abuse and other risky behaviors before they ever happen.

Why do girls need such a campaign? During the 1990s, the gender gap in drug abuse narrowed. Girls exceeded boys in some drug use categories. Adolescent girls were shown to use more stimulants than adolescent boys.

Studies show that girls tend to lose self-confidence and self-worth during these transition years. They often perform less well in academics, participate less in sports, and neglect their own interests.

One million teenage girls get pregnant each year. HIV/AIDS infections are increasing at a faster rate among females than males. Between 1985 and 1994, the National Center for Juvenile Justice reported an increase in arrests of young girls for violent crimes—many of them drug related.

More than 350 national, state, and local organizations support the Girl Power! campaign to help girls resist unhealthy influences and to make positive choices for their lives.[7]

Drug Court Program

Arizona was the first state to begin requiring that all of its nonviolent drug offenders go through drug treatment, rather than go to jail. The Arizona Supreme Court estimated that in its first year of operation, the new program saved state taxpayers more than $2.5 million. The program also helped people overcome addictions and eased the problem of overcrowded prisons.[8]

What Can Be Done?

The problem of designer drugs in our society can be overwhelming. But there are things that can be done to make a difference in fighting abuse of designer drugs.

Dealing With Peer Pressure

Peer pressure is feeling that we need to be like others. Not all peer pressure is bad, but some people in groups do things they would never do on their own.

The Arizona court system was the first to begin requiring that all of its nonviolent drug offenders go through drug treatment, rather than go to jail.

Knowing the Facts.
One of the most important weapons in the fight against drugs is knowledge. To be effective in the fight against drugs, we need to know all we can about drugs and the consequences of abuse.

Developing Self-Respect.
People who have a healthy respect for their bodies are less likely to abuse drugs. A study showed that the percentage of twelve-year-olds who know a classmate who has used an illegal drug increased by 122 percent.

Learning and Practicing Good Decision–Making Skills

The best way to prevent drug abuse is never to start. "Just Say No" is not enough. Young people need to be prepared to deal with exposure to drugs. A good way to make healthy decisions is to use a three-step strategy:

1. Identify the decision to be made.
2. Consider the options.
3. Choose the best option and act upon it.[9]

Daring to Be Different

Role-play with friends and family to practice ways to resist unhealthy influences. Develop a set of "turn down" comments. It is smart to be prepared, should the need ever arise.

Choosing Friends Wisely

Being part of a close-knit group of friends who share positive activities is a powerful way to prevent drug abuse.

Drug-Free Alternatives

There are numerous positive alternatives to drug use. These alternatives build self-esteem and produce a natural high.

Sports and Exercise.
Involvement in sports relieves stress. Running increases endorphin levels. Martial arts activities strengthen the body and mind.

Creative Arts Activities.
Develop creative interests—acting, dancing, drawing, photography, learning to play a musical instrument—as fulfilling ways to spend your time.

Journal Writing.
Writing is a means of letting out anger or frustration. Keeping a journal of one's thoughts and dreams is healthy.

Offering to Help Others.

Volunteer at a soup kitchen. Share talents with residents of nursing homes. Tutor a younger student. Be a good listener. Set an example for friends and younger siblings.

Taking an Active Role in Your School's Drug Education Program.

Write an article for the school newspaper about the dangers of designer drugs. Alert newspapers, radio, and television stations to positive stories that promote drug-free youth. Organize a teen speakers bureau to assist in community prevention programs.

Martial arts is just one of many drug-free activities that help to strengthen the body and mind.

questions for discussion

1. In what ways could you share your knowledge of designer drugs and abuse with others?

2. What impact does the media have on drug abuse?

3. Where would you seek help if someone you know was using drugs?

4. Why do you think parents find it so hard to believe that their child uses designer drugs or any other drug?

5. What do you think accounts for the increase in pre-adolescence drug use?

6. What problems are likely to occur when parents do not set limits on teenagers?

7. What steps should be taken if someone you know starts dealing in drugs?

8. What are some ways of improving the quality and availability of substance abuse prevention and treatment?

9. What effect does making designer drugs have on people and the environment?

chapter notes

Chapter 1. Real-Life Stories

1. Cynthia Hanson, "I Had No Idea My Child Was on Drugs," *Ladies Home Journal*, March 1997, pp. 70, 195.

2. Elizabeth Karlberg, "The Nightmare of Crystal Meth," *Teen*, February 1996, pp. 44–47.

Chapter 2. Social Issues

1. Maggie Keresey, "New Info, New Dangers," *Teen*, September 1996, p. 52.

2. Walter Kirn, "Crank," *Time*, June 22, 1998, <http://www.pathfinder.com/time/magazine> (July 1, 1998).

3. Chris Graves, "The New Drug of Choice: Methamphetamine Explodes Onto Minnesota Scene," *Star Tribune* (Minneapolis, Minnesota), September 27, 1998, <http://www.startribune.com> (September 27, 1998).

4. Mark Shaffer, "Meth Epidemic Is Spreading to Households," *The Arizona Republic*, September 22, 1998, <http://www.azcentral.com/archive/> (September 27, 1998).

5. Chris Graves, "Meth Made in Small Quantities in Clandestine Local Labs," Star Tribune (Minneapolis, Minnesota), September 27, 1998, <http://www.startribune. com> (September 28, 1998).

6. J. William Langston and Jon Palfreman, *The Case of the Frozen Addicts* (New York: Pantheon, 1995), pp. 65–68.

7. Alison Fitzgerald, "Crackdown on 'Designer' Drug of Choice For Kids," *Rocky Mountain News* (Denver, Colorado), December 14, 1997, p. 48A.

8. John Cloud, "Is Your Kid on K," *Time*, October 20, 1997, p. 90.

9. Ibid., p. 90.

10. Judy Monroe, "Designer Drug Dangers," *Current Health 2*, September 1994, p. 13.

11. Drug Enforcement Agency, "Drug Situation in the United States," *DEA Factsheet, 1998*, <http://www.usdoj.gov/idea/factsheet/fact698.htm> (August 20, 1998).

12. National Institute on Drug Abuse, "Costs to Society," *NIDA Infofax, 1998*, <http://www.nida.nih/gov> (August 4, 1998).

13. Office of National Drug Control Policy, "Memo for Americans Who Reject Drug Abuse," 1998, <http://www.whitehousedrugpolicy.gov/about/letter.html> (September 5, 1998).

Chapter 3. Young People and Designer Drugs

1. Jonathan Keane, "Wake Up to the Chemical World," *New Statesman*, January 24, 1997, p. 12.

2. Andrew Ross, "The New Suburban High," *Good Housekeeping*, September 1995, pp. 86–89, 130–131.

3. Burrelle's Information Services, Geraldo transcript, February 13, 1996, pp. 6–7, 22.

Chapter 4. Physical and Chemical Effects of Abuse

1. Jack Schafer, "Designer Drugs," *Science*, March 1985, p. 63.

2. Richard S. Cohen, *The Love Drug: Marching to the Beat of Ecstasy* (Binghamton, N.Y.: Haworth Medical Press, 1998), p. 31.

3. Andrea Kaminski, *Designer Drugs* (Madison, Wis.: Wisconsin Clearinghouse for Prevention Resources, 1998), pp. 13–14.

4. Cynthia Kuhn, Scott Swartzwelder, and Wilkie Wilson, *Buzzed* (New York: W. W. Norton & Company, Inc., 1998), p. 72.

5. Julia Drake, "Drug-Taking a Powerful Undertow to Rave Wave," *The Journal* March/April 1995, p. 9.

6. Kuhn, Swartzwelder, and Wilson, p. 75.

7. Addiction Research Foundation, "Designer Drugs," 1995, <http://www.arf.org/isd/infopak/designer.html> (August 25, 1998).

8. National Institute of Drug Abuse, "Methamphetamine Abuse," *NIDA Capsules*, 1997, <http://www.nida.nih/gov> (September 21, 1998).

9. Jenny De Monte and Jim Rimbach, "Deadly Drug Is Synthetic Heroin," *The Record*, (Hackensack, New Jersey), February 5, 1991, p. C4.

10. Schafer, p. 60.

11. Jonathan Hibbs, Joshua Perper, and Charles L. Winek, "An Outbreak of Designer Drug-Related Deaths in Pennsylvania," *Journal of the American Medical Association*, February 27, 1991, pp. 1011–1013.

12. Michael McCormick, *Designer Drug Abuse* (New York: Franklin Watts, 1989), p. 36.

13. Senate Committee Report on Designer Drugs, July 25, 1985, p. 36.

14. Mark Shaffer, "Arizonan Who Beheaded Son Gets Life Prison Term," *The Arizona Republic*, June 6, 1997, <http://www.azcentral.com/archive/> (September 30, 1998).

15. National Institute on Drug Abuse Research Report Series, "Methamphetamine Abuse and Addiction," 1997, p. 6.

16. Anastasia Toufexis, "There Is No Safe Speed: Three Toddlers' Deaths Spotlight the Nation's Latest Drug Epidemic," *Time*, January 8, 1996, p. 37.

17. Maryann Jensen as told to Nancy Stesin, "I Got Hooked on Drugs," *McCalls*, February 1997, pp. 48, 51, 56–57.

18. Ibid.

19. Kaminski, p. 14.

20. National Institute on Drug Abuse, "Like Methamphetamine, 'Ecstasy' May Cause Long-Term Brain Damage," *NIDA Notes*, 1996, <http://165.112.78.61/NIDANotes/NNVol.11N5/Ecstasy.html> September 17, 1998.

21. Vanessa Grigoriadis, "We Do Need Some Education," *New York*, September 7, 1998, p. 12.

22. Alison Fitzgerald, "Crackdown on 'Designer' Drug of Choice for Kids," *Rocky Mountain News* (Denver, Colorado), December 14, 1997, p. 48A.

23. Winifred Gallagher, "The Looming Menace of Designer Drugs," *Discover*, August 1986, p. 24.

Chapter 5. Fighting Drug Abuse

1. Porter Novelli, "A Communication Strategy Statement," 1998, <http://www.whitehousedrugpolicy.gov/> (September 27, 1998), pp. 2, 18–19.

2. Addiction Research Foundation, "Mic Mac Theatre Group," 1998, <http://www.ccsa.ca> September 27, 1998.

3. Craig Steinburg, "Eight Community-Based Programs Recognized for Outstanding Work in Substance Abuse Prevention," NCADI Reporter, April 13, 1999, <http://www.health.org/> (May 23, 1999).

4. Ibid.

5. Ibid.

6. Addiction Research Foundation, "Teen Challenge Farm, London, Ontario, Canada," 1998, <http://www.ccsa.ca> (May 23, 1999).

7. Substance Abuse and Mental Health Services Administration, "About Girl Power!," 1998, <http://www.health.org/gpower> (November 17, 1998).

8. Christopher S. Wren, "Arizona Finds Cost Savings in Treating Drug Offenders," *The New York Times*, April 21, 1999, <http://www.nytimes.com> (May 24, 1999).

9. Novelli, p. 25.

where to write

Addiction Research Foundation (ARF)
33 Russell Street
Toronto, Ontario
Canada M5S 2S1
(416) 595-6000
<http://www.arf.org>

Boys and Girls Clubs of America
Girl Power!
SAMHSA/CSAP
P.O. Box 2345
Rockville, MD 20847
(301) 443-7531
<http://www.health.org/gpower>

National Clearinghouse for Alcohol and Drug Information
P.O. Box 2345
Rockville, MD 20847
(800) 729-6686
<http://www.health.org>

National Council on Alcoholism and Drug Dependence, Inc.
12 West 21st, 7th Floor
New York, NY 10017
NCA-CALL
<http://www.ncadd.org>

National Families in Action (NFIA)
2957 Clairmont Rd, Suite 150
Atlanta, GA 30329
(404) 248-9676
<http://www.emory.edu/NFIA/>

glossary

addiction—Compulsive need for and use of a habit-forming substance.

analog—A substance that is chemically similar to another.

central nervous system—The brain and spinal cord.

designer drug—A drug that is illegally made in laboratories to mimic the effects of an existing drug.

hallucination—Seeing and/or hearing things that are not really there.

narcotic—A drug used to control pain.

opiate—A pain-killing drug that causes feelings of well-being and produces drowsiness.

stimulant—A drug that speeds up the way the brain works.

transmitter—A chemical messenger in the brain.

further reading

Alvergue, Anne. Ecstasy: *The Danger of False Euphoria.* New York: The Rosen Publishing Group, Inc., 1998.

Clayton, Lawrence. *Designer Drugs.* New York: The Rosen Publishing Group, Inc., 1994.

Grabish, Beatrice R. *Drugs & Your Brain.* New York: The Rosen Publishing Group, Inc., 1998.

Nadelson, Carol C., and Claire E. Reinburg, eds. *Psychological Disorders Related to Designer Drugs.* New York: Chelsea House Publishers, 1999.

Robbins, Paul. *Designer Drugs.* Springfield, N.J.: Enslow Publishers, Inc., 1995.

———. *Hallucinogens.* Springfield, N.J.: Enslow Publishers, Inc., 1996.

Shulman, Jeffrey. *The Drug-Alert Dictionary and Resource Guide.* Frederick, Md.: Twenty-First Century Books, Inc., 1995.

index

A

addiction, 6, 12–13, 33, 40, 46, 51
AIDS, 23, 37, 51
amphetamines, 27–31
anesthetic, 44–45
attention deficit hyperactivity disorder (ADHD), 31

B

brain stem, 35–36

C

CAT, 20–22, 34, 41
central nervous system, 35–36
cerebellum, 7, 35
cerebrum, 7, 35
china white, 8, 12, 32–34
Controlled Substances Act, 28, 33
crank, 6–7, 24, 26, 34, 39, 40
crystal methamphetamine, 5–6, 8, 11–12, 23, 31, 34, 37, 39

D

Drug Abuse Warning Network (DAWN), 22
Drug Enforcement Administration (DEA), 19, 30
drug-free alternatives, 53–54

E

ecstasy, 8, 11, 13–14, 24, 29–31, 34, 41–44

F

fentanyl analogs, 33

G

GHB, 34, 45

H

hallucinogens, 29, 34, 40–44
Henderson, Gary, 27
HIV, 23, 51

I

ice, 31, 34, 37, 39

K

ketamine, 19–20, 26, 44–45

L

Lily, John, 20

M

MDMA, 13–14, 29–31, 34, 41
mescaline, 29–30
methamphetamine, 11–12, 15–17, 20, 23, 31–32, 36–39
Monitoring the Future Study, 48
morphine, 27, 46–47
MPPP, 19
MPTP, 18–19, 34

O

Office of National Drug Policy, 23
opiates, 34, 46–47

P

paranoia, 22, 26, 37
Parkinson's disease, 18
peer pressure, 51
pregnancy, 38
prevention programs, 49–54

R

raves, 19, 29, 44

S

special k, 19, 26, 34, 41, 44
speed, 31, 34, 36, 38–39
spinal cord, 7, 35
stimulant, 20–21, 29, 34, 37–38, 50

T

tango and cash, 32–33
transmitters, 44–45
treatment, 40, 49, 52, 55

W

withdrawal, 39
World War II, 31

X

XTC, 13